To skywatchers and stargazers everywhere.
UK

For Jed and Hudson, the brightest stars in my sky.
A S

Many thanks to Sumant Krishnaswamy for his
patience and assistance. This book could not have
been created without his help.

Text copyright © 2015 by Uma Krishnaswami
Illustrations copyright © 2015 by Aimée Sicuro
Published in Canada and the USA in 2015 by Groundwood Books

Groundwood Books / House of Anansi Press
110 Spadina Avenue, Suite 801, Toronto, Ontario M5V 2K4
or c/o Publishers Group West
1700 Fourth Street, Berkeley, CA 94710

We acknowledge for their financial support of our publishing program the Government of
Canada through the Canada Book Fund (CBF).

Library and Archives Canada Cataloguing in Publication
Krishnaswami, Uma, author
Bright sky, starry city / written by Uma Krishnaswami ;
illustrated by Aimée Sicuro.
Issued in print and electronic formats.
ISBN 978-1-55498-405-3 (bound).—ISBN 978-1-55498-406-0 (pdf)
I. Sicuro, Aimée, illustrator II. Title.
PZ7.K75Br 2015   j813'.54   C2014-905904-3
C2014-905905-1

The illustrations were done in watercolor, acrylic, pencil,
pastel chalk and collage, with digital techniques.
Design by Michael Solomon
Printed and bound in Malaysia

BRIGHT SKY, STARRY CITY

UMA KRISHNASWAMI

Pictures by AIMÉE SICURO

GROUNDWOOD BOOKS
HOUSE OF ANANSI PRESS
TORONTO BERKELEY

Phoebe helped Dad set up the telescopes
outside his store.
She added special effects.
"Mercury, Venus, Earth, Mars, Jupiter, Saturn,
Uranus, Neptune."
Phoebe sang the planet names
as she drew. She thought of them
spinning on their axes,
going round and round the sun,
over and over, forever and ever.

Two of the planets — Saturn and Mars —
would be up in the sky later,
between those buildings.
They'd be up, but Phoebe worried
she wouldn't be able to see them.
Would anyone?
Dad knew where to look, but city lights
always turned the night sky gray and dull.

People hurried past,
hugging themselves against the wind
while Phoebe made her planets —
Mercury–Venus–Earth–Mars–Jupiter–
Saturn–Uranus–Neptune —
spin on the sidewalk.

Street lights blinked on.
Neon signs flashed and flickered.
Up in the sky, something faint
tried to glimmer through.
"What's that star?" Phoebe asked.
"Vega?" said Dad. "Deneb?"
It was hard to tell.

"Where are Mars and Saturn?" said Phoebe.
"Over in the west," said Dad.
"If we were out in the country
we could see them. The city lights
wouldn't spoil the night sky."
But they were not in the country.
"It's not fair," Phoebe said.

She closed her eyes and wished
for all the bright lights to disappear.
All those blinking, flashing, glowing lights
that sent pale fingers up into the sky.
She longed for the city lights to go OUT!
Just for a while. Just to give the night sky a chance.

The wind whistled.
A fat drop fell on Phoebe's nose, another in her hair.
Then more and more, splattering on the sidewalk.
"Sorry, Phoebe," said Dad. "We'd better pack it in."

Rain blurred the lights.
Clouds blotted out the sky.
Dad hurried Phoebe
back into the shop.

Phoebe peered through the window
at her sidewalk solar system
dissolving into chalky streams.

"Maybe we should just go home," Dad said.
But Phoebe did not want to go home.
She wanted a beautiful inky-black night.

Lightning cracked the sky.
Phoebe counted the seconds,
one to ten. Thunder crashed.
"Let's wait for the rain to stop," said Phoebe.
"Could be a while," Dad warned.

"What about Mars and Saturn?" said Phoebe.
Dad just shook his head.

Crash! Boom!
The echoes faded.
But something had changed.
Where were all the lights?

With the city suddenly darkened,
Phoebe and Dad sat in the store,
listening to the rain. At last, at last,
at long,
long last,
the downpour slowed from torrent to shower
to pitter-patter-drip.
Phoebe had never heard anything
so glorious.

When the last drops had fallen,
when the wind had died down
and the last clouds were gone,
Phoebe and Dad ventured outside.

Above the newly washed city,
with the power still out,
glowing, sparkling, gleaming lights
painted the night — some faint, some brilliant,
some clustered together
and some scattering fiercely
through the inky darkness.
Stars in the hundreds, some in constellations
that Phoebe had only ever seen
in pictures.

And there they were,
right where they should be.
Two bright and steady points of light —
Saturn and Mars — close to each other
in the western sky.

People milled around,
talking, pointing, laughing, looking
all at once, all together
under the stars.

Phoebe squinted through the telescope
at Saturn-dazzle —
misty, magical, floating rings,
and the faint dot of the planet's biggest moon.
Somewhere in there, too far to spot,
Phoebe imagined the rest of Saturn's many moons,
including the small rocky one
that she was named for.

Dad turned the telescopes,
focusing on one cluster of stars
and then another.
How deep the night was
and how endless!

Then, adjusting to the darkness,
Phoebe saw something
she'd never seen before —
a pale, gauzy, whitish band,
low in the eastern sky.

"What's that cloud?" Phoebe said.

"The Milky Way," Dad said.
"That's part of our galaxy you're looking at."

Phoebe breathed in the night,
with all its stars and planets.
"What a bright, bright sky," she whispered.
"It's a starry city, all right," said Dad.
And it was.

Soon the lights would come back on,
and everyone would hurry off.
But for a brief time, above the dark city,
there was the bright night sky.
The bright night sky,
with the stars in their constellations
and the planets wheeling in their orbits.

MORE ABOUT OUR NIGHT SKY

Our Solar System

Phoebe draws the solar system on the sidewalk in chalk. She draws the sun, its eight planets, their moons and a few other objects such as asteroids and comets.

For centuries, people observed points of light that seemed to move across the night sky. The ancient Greeks called these objects planets, meaning wanderers. We now know that the planets appear to move across the sky because they are going around the sun in oval paths called orbits.

Ancient people knew only five planets. The Romans named them after their gods: Jupiter, king of the gods; Mars, god of war; Mercury, messenger of the gods; Venus, goddess of love and beauty; and Saturn, father of Jupiter and god of agriculture. Long-ago skywatchers also saw comets with ghostly tails, and meteors, or shooting stars, that seemed to fall from the sky.

In the seventeenth century, the scientist and scholar Galileo Galilei built a telescope with which he was able to see details such as craters on the moon, the moons of Jupiter and sunspots. Better telescopes led to the discovery of more planets. We now know of eight planets that orbit the sun: Mercury, Venus, our own Earth, Mars, Jupiter, Saturn, Uranus and Neptune. Pluto was once considered a planet. Now it is described as a dwarf planet, along with others like Ceres and Eris.

The four planets closest to the sun — Mercury, Venus, Earth and Mars — are called the inner or terrestrial planets because they have solid, rocky surfaces. The

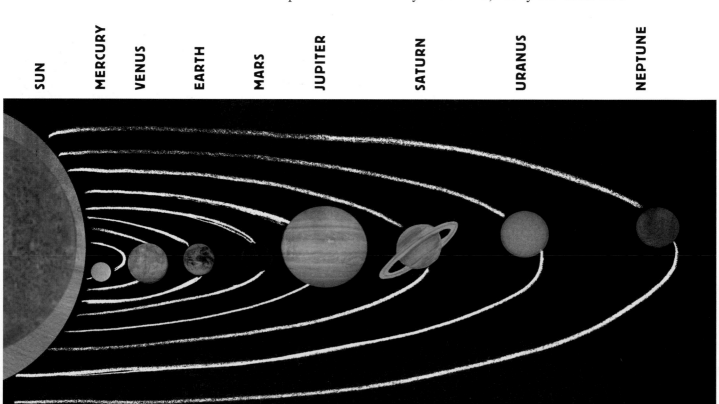

SUN   MERCURY   VENUS   EARTH   MARS   JUPITER   SATURN   URANUS   NEPTUNE

four large planets beyond the orbit of Mars — Jupiter, Saturn, Uranus and Neptune — are called gas giants.

Our sun and all its planets are part of the Milky Way, a flat, disk-shaped galaxy with spiral arms. Our solar system is located in one of the outer spiral arms.

Planetary Conjunctions

Planets move around the sun at different speeds. As a result, sometimes two or more planets can appear near one another in the sky, even though they are really millions of miles apart in space. This is called a planetary conjunction.

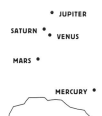

Although the planets are generally visible in both the Northern and Southern Hemispheres, their height above the horizon varies depending on your time zone and on where you are. And so astronomical events like planetary conjunctions may be visible from some areas and not others. Conjunctions of two planets are quite common. It is more unusual to see three or more planets appearing close together. We are of course unable to see conjunctions that may occur during daytime.

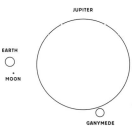

In a rare conjunction in 2002, Saturn, Jupiter, Mars, Venus and Mercury could all be seen in the sky at the same time. In this story, Phoebe sees a conjunction of Saturn and Mars. A conjunction like this one was visible from parts of North America in June 2006.

Moons

Phoebe is especially excited about seeing Saturn, because she's named after one of its moons. Moons are also called satellites. They are usually solid bodies that come in many shapes, sizes and types. Astronomers have found over a hundred moons orbiting planets in our solar system.

Of the inner planets, Mercury and Venus have no

moons. We on Earth, of course, know our moon well. Mars has two small moons, Phobos and Deimos. In the outer solar system, Jupiter, Saturn, Uranus and Neptune have many moons. One of Jupiter's moons, Ganymede, is bigger than the planet Mercury. If it were orbiting the sun on its own, instead of circling Jupiter, we might have to call it a planet. Another of Jupiter's moons, Io, has volcanoes that erupt with sulfur vapors.

Dozens of icy moons orbit Saturn, and astronomers continue to discover new small moons circling the planet. The moon with which Phoebe shares her name is roughly spherical. It rotates on its axis every nine hours and completes a full orbit around Saturn in about eighteen months. Phoebe probably can't see her namesake moon when she looks through Dad's telescope, but she can certainly imagine its shape and its elliptical orbit.

Planetary Rings

Cosmic dust and other small particles trace their own paths around the sun and also around some planets. To us on Earth, these particles may look like rings around the planet. Saturn was once thought to be the only planet with rings. Now we know that ring systems also exist around the other three gas giants — Jupiter, Uranus and Neptune.

Saturn's rings are spectacular. You can see them even through a small telescope. They seem to float magically around the planet. No wonder Phoebe is enchanted by the sight. No wonder scientists are driven to find out more and more about the extraordinary universe in which we live.

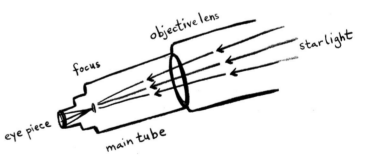

Telescopes

Phoebe's dad sets up telescopes for everyone to look at the bright stars and planets in the suddenly darkened sky. The type of telescope you can buy in a store is called an optical telescope. It is an instrument, built with lenses or mirrors, that allows viewers to see distant objects.

Light Pollution

The night sky in the countryside looks quite different from the sky over a large city. In the country, you can see many more stars and planets. Far from urban lights, you might see part of our own galaxy, the Milky Way, spread out across the sky.

From a big city, you would probably see only a few stars or planets, and they would look faint and dull. This is because of what scientists call light pollution. It is the result of artificial light shining outward and upward into the sky and being scattered in all directions by dust particles in the air. This scattering of light where it is not wanted or needed is called light trespass.

Because of light pollution, people in cities live in a constant human-made glare. As urban areas grow, so does urban sky glow. This brightening of the night skies over cities creates a light dome that can be seen from far away. According to the US National Park Service, city lights from 200 miles (322 km) away wash out the stars in the night sky. The effects of light pollution show up even in pictures taken by satellites from space.

In addition to dimming our view of the stars at night, light pollution is bad for wildlife and plants, and even for human beings. Artificial lights at night can confuse hatching sea turtles and migrating birds. If baby turtles move toward city lights instead of toward the ocean, they may die. Birds that migrate at night may be blinded by bright lights and crash into buildings. When insects are drawn to artificial light, they fail to pollinate night-blooming flowers. Those flowers are then unable to produce seeds, leading whole species of plants to die out. Brightening the night too much can alter our own rhythms of sleeping and waking and may even cause us to become ill.

We do need some light outdoors, so we can find our way around safely at night. But cities are often over-lit, wasting electricity by splashing light uselessly upward. If outdoor lights reflected downward instead, and if we could turn off lights we don't need, we would be better able to see planets and stars, as Phoebe does on the special night in this story.

WORDS FROM THE STORY

axis An imaginary line from pole to pole around which a planet rotates, causing day and night (plural: axes).

constellations Patterns formed by bright stars.

Deneb The brightest star in the constellation of Cygnus, the swan. The diameter of Deneb is about one hundred times the diameter of our sun.

galaxy A system of millions or billions of stars, held together by gravity.

Milky Way The name given by the ancient Greeks to the band of light that is part of our galaxy; the spiral galaxy to which our solar system belongs.

orbit The curved or elliptical path of an object in space (or a human-made rocket) around a star, planet or moon; a repeated revolution of one body around another.

planet A celestial body moving in an elliptical orbit around a star.

star Like our sun, a luminous body of mostly hydrogen gas, held together by gravity and giving off light produced through nuclear energy.

solar system A collection of planets and their moons in orbit around a star.

telescope An instrument containing an arrangement of lenses or mirrors or both, designed to make distant objects appear nearer.

Vega The brightest star in the constellation of Lyra. Vega is three times bigger than our sun.

OTHER BOOKS ABOUT STARS, PLANETS AND THE NIGHT SKY

13 Planets: The Latest View of the Solar System by David A. Aguilar. National Geographic Society, 2011.

Comets, Stars, the Moon, and Mars: Space Poems and Paintings by Douglas Florian. Harcourt, 2007.

Starry Messenger: Galileo Galilei by Peter Sís. Frances Foster Books/Farrar, Straus and Giroux, 1996.

Zoo in the Sky: A Book of Animal Constellations by Jacqueline Mitton, illustrated by Christina Balit. National Geographic Society, 1998.